D1439288

GILLOCK, Libby

Half a world away

Half a World Away

"Coo-ee, Lou-ee."

First published in 2006 by Scholastic Australia
First published in the UK in 2009 by Scholastic Children's Books
Euston House, 24 Eversholt Street
London NW1 1DB
a division of Scholastic Ltd
www.scholastic.co.uk
London ~ New York ~ Toronto ~ Sydney ~ Auckland
Mexico City ~ New Delhi ~ Hong Kong

Text copyright © 2006 Libby Gleeson
Illustrations copyright © 2006, 2007 Freya Blackwood

978 1407 11069 1

1 3 5 7 9 10 8 6 4 2

Half a World Away

By LIBBY GLEESON

Illustrated by FREYA BLACKWOOD

■SCHOLASTIC

Amy and Louis built towers as high as the sky.
They dug holes deep enough to bury bears,
and they saw magical creatures in clouds.

When Amy was in the sandpit
and Louis was on the swing,
she called to him across the yard
with the special word her mother taught her.

"Coo-ee, Lou-ee!"

Louis always came to play.

When Louis was in the dressing-up corner
and Amy was with the play dough,
he called to her across the room
with the same special word.

"Coo-ee, Am-ee!"

Amy always came to play.

And when they were at home, they called
to each other across the fence. "Coo-ee, Lou-ee."

"Coo-ee, Am-ee."   One of them would soon come climbing through the gap with secrets to share.

But one day Amy and her family moved
a long, long way away . . .

. . . to the other side of the world.

Louis stopped building towers,
digging holes, and staring at clouds.
He no longer called to anyone
across the yard, the room, or the fence.

He thought about Amy every day and every night.

In the place where Amy was,
there was nowhere to dig holes or build towers,
and the clouds held only raindrops.

She thought about Louis every night and every day.

"If I call Amy really loudly,
she'll hear me, won't she?"
Louis asked his mum.

His mum shook her head. "Amy is too far away," she said.
"When you are awake in the day, she is asleep at night."

"If I call Amy really, really
loudly, she'll hear me,
won't she?" he asked his dad.

His dad shook his head. "Amy is half the world away," he said.
"When she is awake in the day, you are asleep at night."

"If I call Amy with the loudest
call anyone could ever, ever do,
she'll hear me, won't she?"
he asked his grandma.

"Maybe," his grandma said.
"You can only try."

So Louis spread his arms as wide as he could
and threw back his head.

His cry rang out across the yard,
across the street,
and past the edge of the town.

Louis fell back and stared up at the sky
where clouds were making strange seahorses
and wild, wild dragons.

Across the ocean,
in a city where tall buildings
stretched to the sky,
Amy woke and came sleepily
to breakfast.

"I had a lovely dream," she said.
"I dreamt about Louis
and he called me."

Half a world away,
Louis slept,
smiling in his dream.